# Haffertee Hamster

Haffertee is a toy hamster. Ma
Diamond made him for her little girl,
Yolanda (usually known as Diamond
Yo), when her pet hamster died.

In this book – the first of the Haffertee
stories – Haffertee meets his great
friend Howl Owl, the Diamond family,
and some of the strange and amusing
characters who share their home. He
also learns how he was made – and
why.

The charm of the stories lies in the
funny, lovable character of Haffertee
himself, and in the special place God
has in the affections of Diamond Yo
and her family.

# The Diamond Family

Fran                    Ma

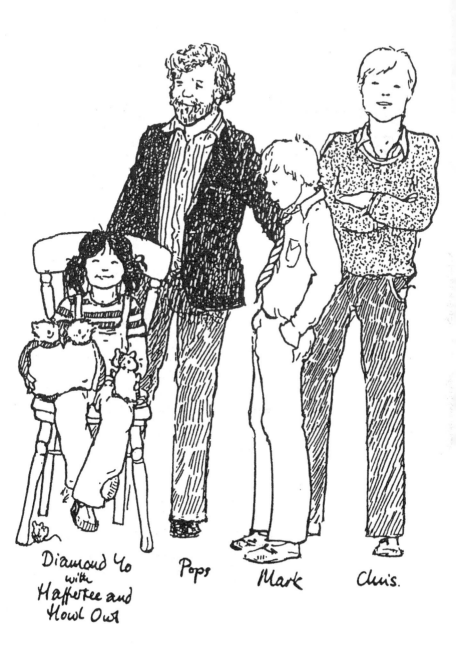

Diamond Yo
with
Haffertee and
Howl Out

Pops

Mark

Chris.

# Haffertee
## Hamster

### Janet and John Perkins

A LION BOOK

Published by
**Lion Publishing plc**
Sandy Lane West, Oxford, England
ISBN 0 7459 2067 5

First edition 1977
New editions 1979, 1982, 1989
Fifth edition published 1991
10 9 8 7 6 5 4

Illustrations by Gillian Gaze

A catalogue record for this book is available
from the British Library

Printed and bound in Great Britain by
Caledonian International Book Manufacturing

# Contents

It all began when Yo's pet hamster died. To cheer her up, Ma Diamond made a ginger-and-white toy hamster. The new Haffertee Hamster proved to be quite a character – inquisitive, funny and lovable. From his home in Yo's bedroom – shared with his friend Howl Owl and a strange collection of toys – he set out to explore Hillside House and meet the family: Ma and Pops Diamond and Yo's older brothers and sister, Chris, Fran and Mark. His adventures at home, at school and in the World Outside are told in eight books of stories: *Haffertee Hamster, Haffertee's New House, Haffertee Goes Exploring, Haffertee's First Christmas, Haffertee Goes to School, Haffertee's First Easter, Haffertee Goes to Hospital* and *Haffertee Goes on Holiday.*

# 1

## The New Haffertee Hamster

Haffertee Hamster was dead.

Diamond Yo was so sad. School was terrible. And going home again would be even worse.

The empty cage . . . the silent wheel . . . and no Haffertee. What could be worse than that? How could she ever go home again?

Diamond Yo was so sad.

But she did go home again – to the empty cage and the silent wheel. And the tears came.

No Haffertee!

The little fluffy, ginger-and-white animal she had brought home from the shop only a few weeks ago was gone.

She could remember the shop quite clearly. Piles and piles of cages and such a strong smell. And there was Haffertee hamster, with no name, sniffing at the wire of his cage.

"Please! Let me take her home," squealed Diamond Yo. "Let me take her home and have her tea."

HAVE HER TEA. That was the name that stuck.

HAFFERTEE. Even though *she* turned out to be a gentleman and not a lady after all.

Mummy and Daddy and God had all been nice that day. But now Haffertee Hamster Diamond was dead. Diamond Yo was so sad.

But Ma Diamond was at home. She put her arm around Yo and said quietly, "Look what I've got."

Through her tears, Yo looked.

What a funny little fellow! Ginger and white. Almost alive he looked. Black whis-

kers twitching, surely. And certainly a smile
on his face.

"This is a new Haffertee," said Ma Diamond gently. "He is only a soft toy really.
I've just finished making him. You have him
now, Yo, and love him."

Yo's face brightened a little. A smile
struggled through. Her hands reached out to
touch.

How soft the new Haffertee felt. How
cuddly!

Slowly at first, then quick and excited, she tickled his whiskers and poggled his ears.

"Haffertee," she whispered. "You *are* a Haffertee."

The tears were gone now. And Haffertee

and Yo were all over the house. Yo showed him everywhere. And before they knew it, it was time for bed.

Haffertee was given a very special place inside Diamond Yo's pillowcase. His head was just poking out, and his whiskers were free. He felt oh so close.

When they were both happily settled in bed, Yo began to sing . . .

Haffertee's warm and in my bed.
On my pillow, near my head.
Haff-er-tee, Haff-er-tee.
My new little soft toy friend.
Thank you, God. Thank you, God.
For my new little soft toy friend.

"What a lovely song," thought Haffertee, as he settled down for his first night in the Diamond family home.

What a lovely song!

# 2

## Haffertee Finds a Friend

Haffertee felt great. He had a warm, soft place just inside Diamond Yo's pillowcase and he belonged to someone. Yes, Haffertee felt great.

And what a lovely house. Yo had shown him all round. The garage, the kitchen, the bedrooms and the loft.

It had been such fun to feel Yo tickling his whiskers and poggling his ears. Now he had a cosy warm feeling inside, and was ready to sleep.

Ssshhhhh . . . Aaaahhhhhh . . .

*"Toowit, toowoo."*
What was that?
*"Toowit, toowoo."*
What *was* that?
Haffertee was suddenly very scared. He wriggled back down inside the pillowcase as far as he could go.

An owl. Could it be an owl? Owls had fierce beaks and sharp claws. But the sound had not been fierce. It had been gentle.

"I'm up here!" said a very deep voice. "Up here on the shelf above the door."

It was a very, very deep voice. Haffertee froze. His eyes stretched wide, trying to see the voice. And there, on the shelf above the door, was . . .

An owl! A big owl! A big, brown owl!

Haffertee swallowed quickly. "Hello! I'm . . ." His voice failed him.

"Hello!" said the very deep voice. "I'm Howl Owl Diamond. Have you come to join the family?"

"Yes," squeaked Haffertee, feeling a little better. "Yes," he squeaked again. "I only arrived today."

"Then welcome," said the owl slowly. "Welcome to Hillside House. There's no need to be frightened of me. We are all friends here. I shall be delighted to have someone to talk to. And I shall be very pleased to show you round." Howl rolled his big eyes and slowly nodded his head.

"What a big bird," thought Haffertee. And he eased himself a little bit further out of his pillowcase to get a better look.

"What do you do?" he said at last.

Howl sat quite still for a moment or two. Then he said, "I sit here on the shelf. I keep quite still, and I think and I watch – and then I know."

"You know what?" asked Haffertee, puzzled.

"I know what's what," replied Howl.

Haffertee turned his head a little to one side and screwed up his face. He was trying to take it all in. There was a short pause. Then, very politely, Haffertee thanked Howl for sitting still and thinking – and he settled back into his pillowcase again.

If Howl knew "what was what", he was a good friend to have. A very good friend to have.

# 3

## Haffertee and the Picture Pattern

When Haffertee woke next morning, the first person he looked for was his friend Howl Owl.

There he was, on the shelf above the door, eyes closed. Haffertee looked all round the room.

There was a piece of paper lying on the floor. It was covered in funny drawings. And along one side Haffertee could see his own name written in big, bold black letters. HAFFERTEE HAMSTER DIAMOND, SOFT TOY.

"That's odd," thought Haffertee. And he pulled himself out of his pillowcase and went over to take a closer look.

He picked the paper up and looked at it this way and that way and the other way.

This way he couldn't understand it.

That way it made no sense.

And the other way was just as puzzling.

"Whatever is it?" he murmured to himself. At least, he thought it was to himself. He had not heard Howl Owl flutter down from the shelf. Howl's deep voice made him jump.

"That's a pattern," said Howl slowly.

"Oh!" said Haffertee quickly, not liking to ask what a pattern was.

"Those are the pictures Ma Diamond used to help her cut out your pieces and put you together."

Haffertee felt rather strange. The idea of being cut out and then put together seemed very odd.

He looked at himself carefully.

He looked at himself sideways and front-ways and upwards and downwards.

He still couldn't see that he looked at all like the drawings on the paper.

"You say Ma Diamond made me?" he squeaked at last.

"Yes," said Howl certainly. "Ma Diamond made you. She drew these pictures of your pieces and then she cut you out. She sewed the pieces all together and she made you. And now that she has made you, she loves you."

"Ma Diamond made me," squeaked Haffertee again. "Ma Diamond loves me?"

"Just like God," said another voice, softly. "Just like God."

Howl and Haffertee turned together to look at the voice.

Diamond Yo was sitting up in bed. Her hair was all mixed up and she was still half asleep. "You two make a lot of noise early on a Saturday morning. You woke me up."

"Sorry," said Howl slowly.

"Sorry," said Haffertee quickly. "But you see," went on Haffertee in a hurry, "I saw this piece of paper with my name on it and I couldn't understand what the pictures

were. Howl has been explaining it all to me. And now you say Ma Diamond is just like God. What do you mean?"

"Well," said Yo gently, "Ma Diamond made you, and God made Ma Diamond. Ma Diamond loves you, and God loves Ma Diamond."

"Ah!" said Haffertee knowingly, "then God must be a Great Maker."

"Yes," said Diamond Yo, after a moment's thought. "Yes, God is a Great Maker. He made everything and everyone."

"And he must be my Grandfather," went on Haffertee happily.

Diamond Yo settled back against her

pillow to think. That sounded funny. But Haffertee was nearly right. "Not your Grandfather," she said. "But you could say God is your Grand Great Father." And she was still thinking how important that was when she heard Haffertee singing . . .

Ma Diamond made me, as you
can see,
From fur and felt and stuffing.
But God made her without any fur.
He made her kind and loving.
So God must be, decidedly,
Greater than Ma by far.
He loves her,
She loves me,
So I have a Grand Great Father.

"Wonderful," thought Haffertee as he finished the song. "Wonderful! I like having a Grand Great Father . . ."

# 4

# Haffertee Finds Out Why

Haffertee wanted to have a word with Ma Diamond. He was very glad to know she had made him. He was delighted that she loved him. But Haffertee wanted to know *why*.

Ma Diamond was easy to find. She was in the kitchen. There was always plenty to do, with Pops Diamond and three children to look after. Food to prepare. Meals to serve. Dishes and plates to wash.

So Haffertee made his way down to the kitchen.

Ma Diamond had just sat down for a quiet cup of tea. Diamond Yo was still in bed! Everyone else was out. So Ma Diamond was all on her own for once.

"Hello Haffertee," she called out, as he came in. "Come up on the table here and talk to me for a little while."

That was just what Haffertee wanted. He climbed up on the table and settled himself

down. Then he took a deep breath and said rather quickly, "Did you draw this picture, Ma?"

He pulled the pattern out from behind him, unfolded it and smoothed it out on the table.

Ma Diamond looked at it. "Yes," she said. "I drew that."

"Why?" asked Haffertee sharply.

It sounded rather rude. But Ma Diamond could see that Haffertee was very anxious about something, so she took no notice.

"Well now," she said. "I thought Howl Owl had explained all that this morning."

"Oh!" said Haffertee in great surprise. He did not know that Ma Diamond had heard him talking with Howl and Diamond Yo.

"Oh!" he said again. "Well . . . er . . . yes. Howl told me that you made me, and he said you love me. I am very glad about that. But . . . but . . . I want to know *why* you made me."

"Ah!" said Ma Diamond slowly. "Now that is a long story. You see, once upon a time we had a real live hamster in the family, and we called him Haffertee. But a little while ago he died. Diamond Yo was so sad. She couldn't bear to look at the empty cage. She couldn't bear the thought of going to school. All day long I tried to think of something to make her happy again. And then I thought of you."

"You thought of me?" echoed Haffertee. "You thought of *me*?"

"Yes," said Ma quietly. "I though of you. I drew a picture of you, and then I made a pattern of your pieces. When I had finished cutting them out I stitched them all together – and there you were . . . all soft and fluffy and cuddly. Diamond Yo was so pleased to see you when she came home. You made her happy again."

Haffertee liked the idea of making Diamond Yo happy. He liked the idea very much. He liked it so much that he was silent for a long time, just thinking about it.

Then he said, "Did you really make me just to make Yo happy?"

"Yes," said Ma, trying hard to convince him. "I made you to make Diamond Yo happy. And because you made Diamond Yo happy, you have made me happy, too."

Haffertee was pleased. That was really something. As he was thinking, Ma began to sing quietly . . .

You were made for happiness,
happiness, happiness.
You were made for happiness,
My little soft toy friend.

Haffertee felt a tear of pure happiness trickle down his nose. He climbed down from the table and back up to Yo's room.

He had made Yo happy. Ma was glad that she had made him. How lovely it was to make people happy!

# 5

## Diamond Yo and the Shadow

Haffertee was warm and snug inside his pillowcase. It had been a wonderful day.

Now it was time to sleep. But there was something troubling him. Well, not exactly troubling him . . . just making him think.

What was Howl Owl doing up there on the shelf above the door? Why was he in the Diamond family?

Just a little bit more thinking. Then Haffertee decided he simply had to find out.

"Yo," he whispered, quietly.

There was no reply.

"Yo," he said again, in a loud whisper.

Still no reply.

Haffertee wriggled down into the pillowcase and began to kick about.

"What are you doing, Haffertee?" said Yo sleepily, easing her head along the pillow, away from the bobbling. "What *is* the

matter?"

Haffertee poked his head out of the pillowcase quickly. "Who made Howl Owl, Yo? And why?" he asked, all of a rush. Yo snorted.

"Not now, Haffertee," she said rather crossly. "I'm half asleep. Can't it wait until tomorrow?"

"Not really," said Haffertee. "I can't get to sleep for puzzling."

Yo knew Haffertee would just go on asking and asking, so she rubbed her eyes and began to think.

"Howl Owl was made for me to cuddle," she said, simply. "Ma Diamond made him, just like she made you. First of all she thought of him, then she drew a picture of him, and then she made him."

Haffertee thought about that for a moment or two. "I see," he said at last. "But why did she do it? How did she come to think of him in the first place? I know why she made me. Why did she make Howl?"

Yo could see there wasn't much chance of going to sleep until the whole matter had been settled. So she took a deep breath and started her story.

"Once upon an evening," she began quietly, "I was sitting in the garden after a lovely day playing in the wilderness, when a dark shadow flew over me."

Haffertee screwed himself into a tight ball. It sounded a bit frightening.

Yo felt the movement and went on. "Yes," she said, "I was frightened, too. I didn't know what the shadow was. I sat as still as still for a moment and waited. The shadow came back and over me again. It seemed very close and very dark and it whirred. I felt all tight inside and I couldn't move."

"Oooooh!" said Haffertee. "Ooooh!"

"Then," said Yo, very slowly, knowing

that Haffertee was listening carefully. "Then I heard another funny noise. 'Toowit! Toowoo! Toowit! Toowoo!' It scared me all over. I didn't know what it was."

Haffertee relaxed, and came further out of the pillowcase. There was a smile on his face.

"I know what that was," he said proudly. "It was an owl."

"Why, yes," said Yo, with some surprise. "But how did you know?"

"Because I was frightened like that too," said Haffertee. "The first night I came. And it was Howl Owl."

"Well I never," said Yo. "You're right! Howl Owl does sing like that sometimes. But that night I'd never heard the sound before, and I was so scared. When Mummy called me in I couldn't say anything. It took me ages to get washed and into bed. And longer still to find my voice again, and tell her what had happened. She was so kind, though. We had our Bible story and said our prayers, and then she stayed and talked for ages and ages. She was singing to me when I fell asleep. I was so glad she stayed. Next morning, when I woke up, there was Howl Owl."

Haffertee was rather taken by surprise. He eased himself right out of the pillowcase and then said, "Oh!"

The two of them were silent for a bit. Then: "Howl Owl there in the morning," Haffertee muttered at last. "Where does he come into the story then?"

"Ah!" said Yo, with a wide smile. "It was a real live whirring owl that frightened me in the garden, you see. Mummy knew that, when I told her what had happened. She thought that the way to stop me being afraid of owls was to make me an owl to know and cuddle. So there he is . . ." She nodded towards the shelf above the door.

"I used to hug him and snuggle him and smooth him and tickle him so much that he

had to ask if he could sit up there on the shelf at nights. So there he is, my Howl Owl friend."

Haffertee was so quiet, Yo thought the conversation was over. She settled down on the pillow gently, ready to sleep.

"Howl Owl was made to help me get over a frightening experience," she murmured, through a yawn.

"And I was made to help you get over a sadness," said Haffertee, into the stillness.

"Why, yes," said Yo, happily. "You *are* clever, Haffertee. You were made to help me get over a sadness and Howl Owl was made to help me get over a fright."

"So we must both be getover people," said Haffertee gaily. Diamond Yo didn't see the twinkle in his eyes but she felt sure it was there.

Haffertee snuggled down inside the pillowcase. He and his friend Howl Owl were getover people. That was a nice Last Thought to sleep on.

# 6

## The Desk-Maker and the Daisies

The whole place was being turned upside down. At least it seemed like that. The bed itself was moving.

Haffertee stretched out of the pillowcase to get a better view of the disturbance.

It was Chris Diamond. All six feet of Diamond Yo's big brother!

"Come on you two," said Chris. "Get out of there now, I want to get started."

Yo was slowly moving up from under the bedclothes. "Come on then, Haffertee," she yawned. "I suppose we had better get up. If Chris wants to get on with something, we had better move."

Haffertee jumped up out of the pillowcase and then down on to the floor. Howl Owl fluttered down from the shelf to join him.

"Let's get out of here," said Howl with a hoot.

"Why?" asked Haffertee in surprise. "What *is* going on?"

He didn't like being wakened up so suddenly in the morning and being shooed out of bed by a big disturbance, even if it was Chris Diamond wanting to get on with something.

"Well now," said Howl slowly. "It's desk-making time, I suppose."

"Desk-making time," said Haffertee. "Desk-making time? What do you mean?"

"Come out here on the landing and watch," said Howl with a knowing smile. "Perhaps you will find out."

The two of them moved out on to the landing.

"Now just stand there and watch," said Howl.

Haffertee did as he was told, and stood there and watched. Chris was very busy moving the furniture about. The bed was pushed over against the cupboards. The chair was put up on the bed and the table pushed against the side of the bed. The pictures were taken down off the walls and

piled on the table. Chris was such a whirl-wind that Yo wasn't much use to him really, although she did try to help.

Downstairs went Chris at last, when the whole room had been changed round. And in no time at all he was back again with a box of tools and a saw and some pieces of wood and Pops Diamond's tin of screws and nails. Chris had rolled back the carpet. Now he put the box of tools, the saw and the pieces

of wood down on the wooden floor. He put
the tin of nails and screws on the table, and
then he started.

He measured this and he measured that
and he measured the other.

He sawed this and he sawed that and he
sawed the other.

He banged here and he banged there.

He fitted that over this and this over
that.

He pushed and pounded and pulled and banged.

And in no time at all, or so it seemed, there was a smart desk fitted in the corner of Yo's room, with some shelves down one side and a nice flat top for Yo to rest her arms on.

Chris had worked quickly and carefully and there it was! A lovely desk made of pieces of wood and screws and nails and a special smooth top. Yo was delighted with it.

"Lovely!" she said, as they put the carpet back down.

"Wonderful," said Ma Diamond, as she helped put the bed and the chair and the pictures back in place.

"Remarkable," said Haffertee to Howl, as the two of them came cautiously back into the bedroom. "Remarkable!"

When the noise of the sweeping had

stopped and the room was quite straight again, Haffertee turned to Yo and said, "However does he do it?"

"Ah!" said Yo happily, "Chris loves making things. He learned a lot about woodwork at school and he has read a lot too. He has made things for his own room. He knows how to use his tools, and so there is my lovely new desk!"

Haffertee looked at it again. It really did look smart. It was lovely and it was new!

Yo began to put some of her books on the shelves. And then she just sat, with her elbows on the desk top, looking very pleased.

"It's just what I wanted," she said happily.

Haffertee climbed up on to the top of the desk to get a closer look. It was firm and smooth and strong. Haffertee liked it very much. He sat down carefully.

"Chris really is very clever to be able to make this, isn't he?" he said at last.

"He certainly is," agreed Yo, and went on happily sitting still. "And have you seen these, Haffertee?" she said, after a long silence. "Aren't they lovely?"

Haffertee looked. Yo was holding a small plastic egg cup with some daisies peeping out over the edge.

"Mummy brought those up to go on the desk top."

Yo picked one of them out and looked at it. "God made that," she said slowly, turning it round and round.

Haffertee watched her for a moment. "Gracious," he said. "Did he really? How long did it take him?"

Yo went on turning the daisy. She couldn't think of an answer to that one.

"It is beautiful," said Haffertee gently. "What sort of tools did God use?"

Yo couldn't think of an answer to that one either.

"Why did he make them?" Haffertee asked, after a pause.

Again there was no answer. The two of them just sat there quietly looking at the daisies. They were both surprised by a voice behind them.

"God made the daisies because he wanted to," said Chris. "He loves making things and he knew you would like them, too!"

# 7

## Mr Jumpastring

Haffertee really felt at home now. It was a feeling he liked. Hillside House was a homey home. It was an interesting home, too.

He was just thinking quietly about that when he heard someone whistling.

After a while the whistling changed to a trumpeting sound.

Then the trumpeting changed to a drumming sound.

The drumming didn't last long either. It soon changed to a soft tinkling sound.

"What strange noises," thought Haffertee, "what *very* strange noises."

He listened carefully. All the sounds were coming from one of Diamond Yo's cupboards. He decided to investigate.

He dropped down off the bed, went over to the cupboard and bent down so that his ear was close to the crack at the bottom of the door.

He could hear someone singing away merrily. The voice was rather squeaky. The song was very happy.

Very soon Haffertee was joining in and singing loudly too. He almost started dancing round the room. Then he stopped singing and looked up at Howl Owl on his perch above the door.

Howl's head was moving from side to side in time with the music. One of his feet was tap-tap-tapping away.

Suddenly the singing in the cupboard stopped, and Haffertee called up to Howl, "Who is that in there?"

Howl chuckled. "Open the door and see," he said.

Haffertee was just a little bit scared. But he pulled open the door and looked inside.

There were several pairs of shoes on the floor. They didn't look as if they could sing.

Then he saw some colourful dresses on hangers. They didn't look as if they could sing either.

He was just beginning to wonder who it could have been, singing in the cupboard

like that, when a high-pitched voice squeaked at him. "What a funny fellow you look!"

Haffertee stood quite still. He wasn't very pleased to be called a funny fellow. Who would dare to give him a name like that?

Something about halfway up the wall inside the cupboard bounced and caught his eye. Now Haffertee knew who had called him a funny fellow.

He was a very funny fellow himself. He was made out of odd pieces of wood, stuck together in a most unusual way. His feet were like small boats and his nose was enormous. But his eyes were soft and gentle. There was a piece of bright material wound round his body like a bandage and his arms stuck out through it. The top of his head was attached to a long piece of black elastic. And he bounced up and down on it as though he was dancing.

Haffertee watched him bounce for a moment or two and then he said, "Hello! I'm Haffertee Hamster Diamond."

"Hello," said the little wooden man. "My name is Mr Jumpastring and I am a friend of Diamond Yo."

"I am too," said Haffertee. "I've just come to live at Hillside House." Then he asked politely, "What do you do?"

"Oh!" said Mr Jumpastring, "I just dance and sing and dance and sing. I love dancing and singing."

Haffertee thought that sounded nice.

"Could you show me how to dance and sing?" he said suddenly.

Mr Jumpastring did an extra high jump on his elastic. "I should love to," he said excitedly, "just step inside and we'll see what we can do."

Haffertee stepped inside the cupboard and closed the door.

Mr Jumpastring showed Haffertee how to hop and skip and jump, and how to twist and turn and swivel. Haffertee learned how to open his mouth wide when he sang and how to make a sound like a whistle and a sound like a trumpet and a sound like a drum. He had a wonderful time doing all the things his feet could manage. And he was very sorry when they had to stop. He wanted the lesson to go on for ever.

But at last he said "Thank you," and

"Goodbye," to Mr Jumpastring and came back out of the cupboard.

After all those lessons he found that his throat was rather sore and his legs were aching. But he was tingling all over. It had been *great* fun.

As he looked round the room, he saw Diamond Yo sitting at her desk. There was a merry smile on her face.

"I can see you enjoyed your visit to Mr Jumpastring," she said happily. "I could hear you singing together right over here."

"I like Mr Jumpastring," Haffertee said firmly. "He is great fun."

"He certainly is," said Yo slowly. "He certainly is. And do you know, Haffertee, he was carved out of wood by one of the boys at Pops Diamond's school. Pops liked him so much that he brought him home for me to play with. I fixed his elastic on the rail in the cupboard and he's been dancing and singing in there ever since. If ever I feel sad, I just open the door and watch him dance and listen to him sing. He always cheers me up."

Haffertee thought about that for a moment or two. It was rather nice to have a friend like that around, someone who could always cheer you up.

"What was he made for?" asked Haffertee, with a little frown.

"Mr Jumpastring was made for fun," said Yo proudly. "All for fun."

Haffertee smiled. He knew how right she was!

# 8

## Birds on the Window-sill

Haffertee was enjoying sitting on the smooth, flat top of Diamond Yo's new desk. It was a nice place to sit, and just high enough for him to be able to see out of the window.

And outside the window, just at that time, was a choir of chirruping birds. Little ones and bigger ones. All sitting happily on the window-sill, enjoying the warm sunshine and chirping noisily away.

Haffertee had never seen so many birds before. There they were, all lined up and feathery, singing away and singing away.

It was quite a sight.

It was quite a sound.

And Haffertee liked them both.

Suddenly there was a great white whoosh! Mrs Ellington Purrswell had arrived on the desk top. The birds were gone like a flash, wings whirring and heads stretching forward. The sight of a big white cat was enough.

Haffertee was flat on his back. That great white whoosh had knocked him over. He struggled back to his feet.

"You really must be more careful," he said sharply, as he brushed himself down and set his whiskers straight again.

Mrs Ellington Purrswell looked at him closely. Haffertee let her look. He had met Mrs Ellington Purrswell before, so he wasn't frightened. Even so, to have her sitting there in front of him like that sent a little shiver of uncertainty running down his back fur.

He pulled himself up to his full height and said again, "You really must be more careful."

"I'm sorry, Haffertee," said Mrs Purrswell, at last. "I was looking for some food for my kittens."

"Birds aren't for eating," thought Haffertee. "What will she do with the feathers?" But before he could go any further with that kind of thinking, he was flat on his back for the second time!

Three more white whooshes had arrived on the desk top. The Purrswell kittens.

Dominic, Tina and Smudge were growing fast. And they were eating anything and everything they could find to eat. They were roaming all over the place with their mother. They'd just roamed all over Haffertee!

He got up again and was just going to say – for the third time – "You really must be more careful," when the four cats shot off the desk top and out of the room.

Haffertee settled his fur once more, and straightened his whiskers yet again. Then he stood quite still. Someone was laughing close by.

He turned round slowly and looked.

Diamond Yo was sitting on her bed and chuckling away.

"Why are you laughing at me?" he asked, feeling just a little bit cross.

"You did look funny being knocked over twice by the Purrswell family," said Yo with a smile.

"Hummmm," said Haffertee. Perhaps it had looked rather funny. He hadn't been able to see much.

Yo's smile faded. "I'm sorry I laughed, Haffertee," she said. "Are you hurt?"

"No, not really," said Haffertee, smiling himself now. "Where did those kittens come from?"

"From downstairs," said Yo.

"No! I don't mean where did they come from before they came up here. I mean, how were they built?"

Yo's smile returned. Haffertee did ask some funny questions! He was thinking about her desk. She began to think very carefully.

"They weren't really built, Haffertee," she said gently. "You see, they began inside Mrs Ellington Purrswell. She made them there. And when she had made them big enough and strong enough, she let them come out and they were born. They were born, Haffertee, not built."

Haffertee thought that was a wonderful way to make kittens. He sat and thought about it for what seemed a very long time. Then he said, "Were you born, Yo?"

"Yes," said Yo, happily. "I began inside Ma Diamond. I grew there and when I was big enough and strong enough, I came out and I was born. God planned it that way."

There was another long silence, while Haffertee thought about that.

"So some things are cut out and stitched," he said slowly. "Some things are built. And some things are born. Is that right?"

"Well, yes," said Yo. "You could say that."

The twittering and chirruping was back outside the window. The long line of birds was on the sill again. Haffertee and Yo looked and listened and thought.

"How did *they* start?" asked Haffertee, puzzled about feathers again.

"They came out of eggs," said Yo.

That was almost too much for Haffertee. He settled down on the smooth, flat desk top and looked at the birds. He was thinking hard.

"Eggs," he muttered. "What a lot of different ways to begin!"

# 9

## Rabbearmonklio

Howl Owl was going to the Toy Cupboard Music Party. He wasn't much of a one for parties, but he loved meeting his friends and talking over all that had happened during the week.

This week Haffertee Hamster had happened! Howl had invited Haffertee to the party and the little hamster was very excited.

When Howl Owl fluttered down from the shelf above the door Haffertee had been ready for a long time.

"Come on," said Howl. "We mustn't be late."

The two of them moved across the carpet towards the cupboards. The Toy Cupboard was very clearly marked. The letters were stuck on the outside of the door, and they were very big. Diamond Yo had drawn them and coloured them and cut them out herself.

Howl opened the door carefully. It squeaked!

"SSSSSSSHHHHHHH!!!!!!!"

Everybody inside the cupboard said, "SSSSSSSHHHHHHH!!!"

Howl and Haffertee stood absolutely still.

"Come in quietly," said a friendly voice. "Close the door and sit down."

The two friends went in on tip-toe and sat down. There were lots and lots of toys in the cupboard, sitting on the floor and standing round the walls. They were all watching a strange-looking creature walking about in the middle of the floor with a baby doll in his arms. He had the ears of a rabbit, the cuddly body of a teddy bear, the merry face of a monkey, and a lion's long tail. And he was singing very, very softly.

Haffertee had to strain his ears to hear the words of the song. It was a gentle lullaby about Dreamland. At last, the baby doll fell fast asleep and the strange creature put the doll down carefully on a pile of clothes in the corner. There were lots of other babies there and they were all fast asleep.

"Now we can begin," he said.

A little monkey in a bright red jacket took a mouth-organ out of his pocket and began to play a merry tune. Everyone got up straight away and began to hop and skip in time to the music.

A toy soldier started to bang on his drum and two little gnomes whistled away happily. Very soon the whole floor was covered with skipping toys – ones and twos and threes and more. It was such a merry sight. The toys were running and jumping here and there and everywhere, with him and her and everyone.

"Come on," said Blue Fluffy Rabbit. "Come and play catch with us."

So Haffertee did. What fun he had rushing and dashing and twisting out of reach.

He played Merry-go-round with the rabbits.

He marched in line with the toy soldiers.

And he twisted and turned and tumbled
with the clowns.

He got rather mixed up with the firemen playing Musical Ladders, but he loved every minute. He met so many new friends, and played so many new games, and sang so many jolly songs that he was all jumbled up when the lullaby singer said they must stop because it was getting late.

Howl and Haffertee said "Good night" to everyone and shut the cupboard door behind them. They wandered slowly and thoughtfully over to the bed, chattering away as friends do at the end of a happy evening.

"Thank you for inviting me," said Haffertee. "It was such fun."

Howl smiled. He had been very proud of his new friend at the party.

"Tell me, Howl," Haffertee went on. "Who is that strange creature who sang the lullaby?"

"That," said Howl Owl proudly . . . "that is Rabbearmonklio. He is a mixture. He has the ears of a rabbit, the body of a bear, a monkey's merry face and a lion's long tail. Pops Diamond made him for all the family one Christmas time, and we've never discovered what he's really supposed to be. He takes care of all the toys in the Diamond family. If ever you are angry or worried and want someone to soothe you, go to Rabbearmonklio. He knows some lovely songs and poems, and he tells the most marvellous stories."

Haffertee was listening carefully. He was very glad he had met Rabbearmonklio. He would certainly go to see him in the Toy Cupboard one of these days.

Howl was getting ready to fly back to his place above the door. "Good night Haffertee," he said, as he spread his wings and flew off. "Good night."

Haffertee scrambled up on to the bed.

"Did you enjoy yourself?" asked a sleepy Yo.

"It was wonderful," said Haffertee, with a contented smile. "Just wonderful!

Yo . . .," Haffertee hesitated.

"Yes, Haffertee."

"Yo, how does Rabbearmonklio manage to make other people so happy when he's so mixed up himself?"

"Ah!" said Yo. "Rabbearmonklio was made for other people. He doesn't think about himself at all."

Haffertee snuggled down into the pillowcase and closed his eyes. It had been a very full day.

# 10

## Haffertee Belongs

Diamond Yo was suddenly very much awake. There seemed to be no reason for it. It was still quite dark. She could just make out the shape of her clock by the side of the bed but she couldn't see the time.

Yo switched on her bedside lamp. "Goodness me," she yawned to herself. "It's only five o'clock."

There had been other times when Yo had woken up early.

Once she'd had a very bad cold. Ma Diamond had given her a hot drink and a special back massage before she went to sleep. But the cold had made her snuffly and she'd woken up very early in the morning.

Then there was the night before her birthday, when she knew she was going to be given a kitten. There had not been much sleep that night. She was far too excited.

But now . . . this morning . . . there

seemed no reason at all for her to be awake so suddenly and so early.

Yo moved her legs under the bedclothes. Her legs were all right. She'd sometimes woken up with pins and needles. But there were no pins and needles this morning.

Yo looked up at the shelf above the door. Howl Owl was sleeping away happily enough.

Then she turned to look at her pillow. Now Yo knew why she had woken up so early this morning.

Haffertee was gone!

Her dear friend Haffertee Hamster was missing.

Yo began to feel inside the pillowcase, just to make sure he hadn't snuggled right down at the other end.

There was no feel of him.

She tried sliding her hand underneath the pillow itself.

He wasn't there. Where could he have gone.

She struggled up out of bed and pulled the bedclothes back. Perhaps Haffertee had slid down inside the bed. But he wasn't there either.

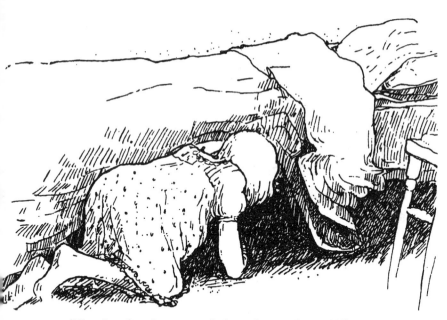

Yo looked round in despair. Wherever could he be? After a moment's thought she decided that perhaps he had fallen down behind the pillow and on to the floor. So she pulled up the bedclothes that were hanging over the side, and bent down to look under the bed.

At first there seemed to be nothing at all. It was all very dark.

Then when her eyes had got used to the dimness, Yo saw him. Right there in the corner, against the leg of the bed and curled up in a tight little furry ball. It was Haffertee.

Yo was so pleased to see him. She knelt down beside the bed and put her hand out to touch him, calling his name softly.

Slowly the little furry ball unwound and Haffertee's face appeared. He had been crying. He did look sad.

Yo lifted him up gently from under the bed and put him on the pillow. He was a sorry little hamster, with his fur all wet and draggled with tears.

"What is the matter, Haffertee?" Yo asked quietly. "Why have you been crying?"

It was some time before Haffertee would answer. Then he said very sadly ". . . I don't know why."

"Was the Toy Cupboard party too much for you?" asked Yo. "Perhaps you got over-excited?"

"Perhaps it was that," sighed Haffertee.

"Perhaps it was." He certainly had been very excited and very tired.

"Did anyone upset you?" asked Yo gently. "Was someone cross with you or anything like that?"

"No," said Haffertee. "I trod twice on Rubber Duck's webbed toes. But I said I was sorry and she wasn't cross."

"Well then," said Yo, trying very hard not to make Haffertee cry again. "What do you think is the matter?"

Haffertee was quite still. Why was he so upset?" He just couldn't put it into words. Then at last he said, "I think it's because there are so many of us here in the Diamond family. I'm afraid I might get lost."

Yo wanted to laugh . . . but she knew better. Haffertee was really worried that he'd be lost among so many new friends. He wouldn't have crawled into that corner under the bed and curled himself into a tight little ball if he hadn't been really worried.

Yo had kept her hand around him, and now she began to stroke him. She poggled his ears with her little finger, and gave him a very special squeeze.

"Haffertee," she said, quietly. "Do you

remember when you first came to Hillside House? I was so sad because I'd lost the live Haffertee. Do you remember how you helped me get over all that sadness and became my very special friend? Well, you still *are* my very special friend, and I love you very much. No matter how many new faces there are in the family – no matter how many nice new friends you and I may meet – you will always be my very special friend, and I will always love you."

You could almost feel the warm glow of happiness that started from Haffertee's toes and moved on all the way through him, until even his ears were burning. And somewhere in the middle of all that happy tingle, Haffertee heard himself say, "Thank you, Yo. Thank you very much."

Then, as he settled back on to the pillow he heard Yo singing:

Haffertee's warm and in my bed.
On my pillow, near my head.
Haff-er-tee, Haff-er-tee.
My dear little soft toy friend.

Haffertee closed his eyes and slipped

slowly into Dreamland. Everything was all right again now. He knew exactly where he belonged.

THE HAFFERTEE STORIES
Janet and John Perkins

Haffertee is a soft-toy hamster. Ma Diamond
made him for her little girl, Yolanda (usually
known as Diamond Yo), when her real pet
hamster died.

These books tell the adventures of the
inquisitive, amusing and lovable Haffertee
Hamster. Each book is illustrated with line
drawings and contains ten short stories, ideal
for bedtime reading or reading aloud.

ISBN 0 7459 2067 5    *Haffertee Hamster*
ISBN 0 7459 2070 5    *Haffertee's First Christmas*
ISBN 0 7459 2072 1    *Haffertee's First Easter*

TALES FROM THE ARK and
MORE TALES FROM THE ARK
Avril Rowlands

Mr Noah could not sleep. He lay in bed,
listening to the wind howling round outside,
and the snuffles and grunts of the animals
inside, and he talked to God.

'Listen, God,' he said. 'It's not too late.
You need a lion-tamer for this job, or a big
game hunter, or at least a zoo keeper. I'm
very grateful that you want to save me and
my family, but I'm not cut out for the job.

'And I'll tell you something, God,' Mr
Noah went on. 'I'm scared of spiders and
we've got two on board!'

Two original and often hilarious books which
tell just what might have happened on board
Noah's Ark.

ISBN 0 7459 2375 5  *Tales from the Ark*
ISBN 0 7459 3035 2  *More Tales from the Ark*

THE ANIMALS' CHRISTMAS
& OTHER STORIES
Avril Rowlands

A donkey entered the stable. On his back was
a young girl. An older man followed on
foot…

'Humans?' spluttered the ox. 'Staying in
my stable? Well, I'm speechless!'

'Thank goodness for that,' said the goat.

On the first Christmas night events in the
stable in Bethlehem were far from ordinary.
Share the fun, joy and wonder of Christmas
in this original collection of animal stories.
Its twelve tales feature animals of all kinds—
sheep and snakes, cats and camels, dormice
and donkeys, and many more besides.

ISBN 0 7459 3699 7

THE KING NEXT DOOR
Alan MacDonald

'And Jesus expected all those people to share
your lunch? Silas, that is without doubt the
biggest whopper you've ever told me. When
are you going to stop making up these
ridiculous stories?'

'But I'm not making it up this time, Mum.
It's true! Jesus made it happen. I don't know
how. Andrew says Jesus is a king. A king can
do anything, can't he?'

In this new collection, ten familiar Bible
stories are retold in the words of those who
met Jesus for themselves.

ISBN 0 7459 3897 3

All Lion books are available from
your local bookshop, or can be ordered
direct from Lion Publishing. For a free
catalogue, showing the complete list of
titles available, please contact:

Customer Services Department
Lion Publishing plc
Peter's Way
Sandy Lane West
Oxford OX4 5HG

Tel: (01865) 747550
Fax: (01865) 715152